For Betty

First published in 2022 in Great Britain by
Barrington Stoke Ltd
18 Walker Street, Edinburgh, EH3 7LP

www.barringtonstoke.co.uk

Text © 2022 Tony Bradman
Illustrations © 2022 Tania Rex

A CIP catalogue record for this book is available
from the British Library upon request

ISBN: 978-1-80090-050-9

Printed by Hussar Books, Poland

CONTENTS

1   Storm from the East   1

2   Sounds of Battle   10

3   Lost in the Woods   19

4   Nothing But Hate   29

5   Blood on Our Hands   38

6   The Road of Tears   48

7   Full of Life   60

    Historical Note   69

"If the dead could speak,

there would be no more war."

– HEINRICH BÖLL

Chapter 1

Storm from the East

East Prussia, Germany – late January 1945

Bruno Beck stood in the doorway of his house and listened to the booms of big guns somewhere beyond the village. He had heard them for the first time early that morning – just a few hours ago. The sound had been distant then but had grown louder. The fighting was closer already.

The street was full of people – Bruno's neighbours running around and shouting. Families were loading all sorts of things onto

carts or horse-drawn wagons. There were
tables and chairs, lamps and vases, boxes and
trunks of clothes. But many people were fleeing
from the village with just a bag or suitcase.
Mothers carried babies and tried to hold on
to toddlers. Grandparents were with older
children. But there were no young men. They
were all in the Army, fighting elsewhere.

"Hurry up, Mother!" Bruno yelled. "We must
leave *now!*"

"I know, I know!" his mother replied. She
came out of the sitting room and stood beside
him in the doorway. Bruno was eleven and
almost as tall as her. They looked alike too.
Both of them were slim and had fair hair, but
her eyes were brown and Bruno's were pale
blue.

"I was trying to think if we might need
anything else on the journey ..." his mother said.
"But you're right, Bruno – I suppose we shouldn't
hang around any longer."

They stepped outside, and Mother locked the door behind them. Bruno wondered if they would ever return to their home, but he didn't ask her. Mother would probably smile and answer, "Of course!" despite thinking the same thing. Bruno was scared and hated leaving, yet they had no choice. He knew Mother was scared too, but she wouldn't admit it – she wanted to stay strong for him.

Bruno took Mother's hand, and they joined the stream of people and wagons passing along the road at the end of the street. The sky was grey, the fields around the village were covered in snow, and it was very cold. Bruno was glad he had a thick coat, a woollen hat and gloves, and good boots. Mother always made sure he had proper, warm clothes, even with everything rationed because of the war.

Mother was wearing a brown coat, walking boots and a dark-green hat with a wide brim. Bruno carried a rucksack stuffed with as

much as he could get into it. He had packed
a spare pair of socks, a family photograph
from the sideboard, a map of Germany in
case they needed it, a loaf of bread, a flask of
water. Mother carried a small suitcase and a
handbag for her make-up, their ration cards and
identity papers.

"It shouldn't take too long to get to the
station," Mother said. They were trudging
behind a wagon full of children. "I only hope the
trains are still running ..."

Bruno hoped so too. They were going to
walk to the station in Königsberg, the nearest
city. It wasn't far from their village, and in
normal times they would have gone there by
bus. But the Army had taken the buses to carry
more soldiers to fight. Mother's plan was to get
a train out of Königsberg and escape from the
fighting. She wanted to get to the city of Kiel,
near the northern border with Denmark.

Bruno's father had grown up in Kiel, and Bruno's grandparents still lived there. Bruno had fond memories of them, despite not having seen them for two years. But he could barely remember Father. The war had begun in 1939, when Bruno was six – five years ago. Father had soon been called up for the Army. Bruno and Mother hadn't seen much of him after that. He'd sent postcards, but he'd only come home on leave a few times, and the last time had been nearly three years ago.

Adolf Hitler, the leader of Germany, had been telling the German people for years that they were surrounded by enemies. It meant the German Army had to fight lots of countries in Europe when the war began – Poland, Norway and Denmark, Belgium, Holland and France, Britain. Yet it seemed as if Germany couldn't lose, and soon it had taken most of Europe.

Then Hitler decided to invade Russia and declare war on America – two of the biggest and most powerful countries in the world. Most Germans hadn't been very worried, not after all the early victories in other countries. The German people thought Hitler was a genius who knew how to win wars. But things soon began to go wrong.

British and American planes bombed German cities, blowing them to pieces and killing thousands of people. The city of Kiel suffered badly – Bruno's grandparents were lucky not to be killed. In June 1944, the British and American armies landed in France, and before long the German Army was getting beaten there. By the end of 1944, the German Army had been pushed right back to its own western borders. And the Russians kept winning battles, eventually forcing the German Army out of their country too.

It was now the beginning of 1945, and the Russians were invading Germany like a great storm from the east. They had done terrible things in the first German village they attacked, killing women and children, and setting the houses on fire. Bruno had seen some awful pictures in the newspaper Mother always read. So it wasn't a surprise that everyone in eastern Germany was panicking. They were desperate to escape before the Russians arrived. Bruno wished he and Mother hadn't left it so late.

Hitler was still saying Germany would win. Bruno wasn't sure about that, despite knowing you weren't supposed to say so. The secret police arrested people who doubted that Germany would win, and the German Army hanged soldiers who ran away from the fighting.

There were rumours the Army had also done terrible things in Poland and Russia and elsewhere ... All Bruno wanted was for his family to be together again, safe and happy. Yet he and Mother didn't know where Father was, or even if he was still alive.

A buzzing noise interrupted Bruno's thoughts. Two fighter planes were heading in their direction.

"Don't worry – they're ours!" an old man shouted. But Bruno felt a jolt of fear. The planes had red stars painted on their wings – they were Russian!

"Run, Mother!" Bruno yelled, grabbing her arm. The planes were close now, their engines roaring. Everyone else saw the danger too. People screamed and ran for their lives. Bruno was knocked over in the stampede and lost his hold on Mother. He screamed too, calling for her, but she was lost in the crowd.

The fighter planes opened fire with their machine guns: RAT-A-TAT-TAT-TAT! Bruno lay on the road, terrified. He covered his head with his arms and screamed even more.

And when he finally looked up ... he saw that Mother had been hit.

Chapter 2

Sounds of Battle

Bruno got to his feet and ran over to Mother. She was lying very still and her face was pale. Her eyes stared at the sky but didn't see anything. Bruno fell to his knees and took Mother's hand, holding it tightly against his lips. Tears ran down his cheeks.

"She's dead," someone said, roughly pulling Bruno to his feet. It was the old man who had shouted about the planes. "You will be too if you don't get out of here!"

"Leave me alone!" Bruno screamed, pushing the old man away. In the space of a few seconds, everything had changed. Now the road was a picture of utter horror. Many people had been killed and there was lots of wailing for dead mothers and fathers and children. A badly wounded horse was struggling to stand up. Further along the road a wagon was on fire, the red flames leaping high and thick smoke rising up from it.

"Don't be stupid, boy!" the old man yelled. "The Russians are coming!"

Bruno was confused. Did the old man mean the planes were coming back? Bruno could hear the sound of engines, but these ones seemed different somehow, with a clanking noise ... Bruno remembered the sound of the Army's tanks clanking on their tracks past the village last year. He looked round and saw five tanks coming across the field. But they had red stars painted on their turrets, not German crosses –

these tanks were Russian! Suddenly the tanks
started firing their guns.

There was a terrific BOOM! as the first shell
landed, then another and another – BOOM!
BOOM! Dust and stones and bits of tarmac fell

on Bruno, and black smoke rose up over the road. Two German tanks appeared on the other side of the snowy field and started shooting at the Russians. Dozens of Russian soldiers were advancing as well. They walked steadily in a line, firing their rifles and machine guns. Bruno thought he saw some dogs running in front of them.

The old man grabbed Bruno's arm and started to drag him away. Bruno kicked and struggled, but the old man was strong and ignored Bruno's protests. They hadn't got far when there was another BOOM! – and the old man just seemed to vanish. After that came explosions and machine-gun fire and people screaming. Bruno ran as fast as he could, at last coming to the edge of a dark wood. He plunged into it, crashing past the undergrowth till he tripped and fell.

Bruno lay there for a moment, the breath knocked out of him. Then he crawled forward on his hands and knees across the snow and dirt and dead leaves. After a while he came to a tree that had fallen, and he slid into the big hole left by the roots. Bruno huddled down, trying to make himself as small as possible, and put his hands over his ears. But he could still hear the explosions and machine guns and people screaming ... And then he heard a new noise that made his stomach churn with terror.

Something – or somebody – was heading in his direction, running at speed, crashing past the undergrowth like Bruno had. It was a large black dog, Bruno saw, as it raced ever closer and flung itself into the hole. Bruno felt even more terrified, certain the dog was going to attack him. He scrambled backwards away from it, but the beast left him alone.

The dog lay panting, its sides heaving, its eyes rolling wildly, its big red tongue lolling out. Bruno realised the poor creature was just as scared as he was.

The dog was wearing a strange vest that covered most of its body. There were several pockets on each side of the vest, all of them stuffed with some sort of clay. At least that was what Bruno thought it was to begin with. Then he remembered reading in Mother's newspaper that the Russian Army used dogs as suicide bombers. He'd read they strapped explosives to dogs and sent them running at German soldiers or tanks to blow them up. Bruno had thought it couldn't be true, but now he knew it was.

He started to shake in fear. He should get as far away from this dog as possible, he thought – even if that meant getting caught in the battle on the road again. If Bruno stayed and the explosives went off, he would be killed instantly. He noticed the dog was shaking too, and staring at him, locking its eyes onto his. The dog's eyes were beautiful and brown, and reminded him of Mother … And as soon as Bruno thought of her, he knew he simply couldn't abandon the dog.

The vest was only tied to the dog with a few
straps and buckles. Bruno carefully eased it
off the dog, his hand shaking with fear at the
thought of the explosives. At last he threw the
vest as far from the hole as he could. He ducked
below the rim of his hiding place before the

vest landed – but there was no BOOM! Bruno breathed a sigh of relief and lay down beside her – he had realised she was a girl dog when he had removed the vest. She licked his hand and whimpered and pressed herself close to him.

"There, there," Bruno said softly, trying to soothe the dog and stop her shaking. The sounds of fighting faded, yet Bruno still felt just as afraid. His mind began to fill with pictures of Mother lying on the road, the life gone from her eyes. Soon he was sobbing. He couldn't believe she was dead, but it was true. It had happened so fast – she had been alive and then she wasn't, like a candle flame being snuffed out.

Now it was the dog's turn to try to soothe Bruno. She nuzzled at his face, licking his tears away, her rough tongue rasping over his cheeks. Her breath was hot, and Bruno realised he was beginning to feel very cold. He wished this was all a nightmare, that Mother was alive and that he was safe at home. But it was real, and now he began to worry that his own life was still in danger in a different way ...

The short winter afternoon was nearly over. The sky was growing dark, the shadows under the trees thickening. Bruno knew the freezing cold of a winter's night could kill you. Maybe it would be easier to give up and let himself die, he thought. This was all too difficult and frightening to deal with ... But the dog whimpered at Bruno again, as if she knew what he was thinking. Then she started scrabbling in the dead leaves that covered the floor of the hole, burrowing underneath them.

Bruno watched and decided he didn't want to die just yet. So he helped the dog. Soon they were snuggled down together, hidden from the world.

He slept badly, and his dreams were full of blood and fire and red stars.

Chapter 3

Lost in the Woods

Bruno called the dog Frida. The name popped into his mind when he woke at dawn. He had no idea where the name had come from, or what kind of dog she was. She had a smooth black coat, a long, narrow muzzle, big pointed ears that stuck straight up and a short, strong tail. Frida was Russian, of course, and Bruno only spoke German, but she seemed to understand everything he said to her.

"Thank you, Frida," Bruno whispered, hugging her. She licked his face and wagged her

tail. "I wouldn't have survived the night without you keeping me warm."

More snow had fallen, and they had been only partly sheltered under the roots of the fallen tree. Bruno could see his breath in the freezing air, and he had never felt so cold. His mind was still filled with the horrors of the day before. He felt guilty that he had run away. The thought of Mother lying alone on the road was too much, and he started crying again. But that was no help. He had to go back to her.

Bruno would need some breakfast first, and so would Frida. He had never had a dog, but he knew how to look after one – there had been plenty in the village. He took the loaf of bread from his rucksack and tore pieces off for Frida and himself. He poured water into his cupped hand for Frida to lap up, and he drank from the flask. Then he returned the loaf and flask to the rucksack, pulled it onto his back and scrambled out of the hole.

Bruno hurried off, his boots sinking into the deep snow. Frida followed, keeping close to him. She seemed happy that they were together, and he realised he liked it too. It made him feel less alone. At least he had someone to talk to.

"I should try to bury Mother," Bruno said quietly to Frida after a while. She looked up at him. "Perhaps the Russians have gone and I'll find someone to help me."

They weren't a religious family, but he should probably say a prayer for Mother too, he thought. Bruno knew he'd been baptised, but Mother had stopped taking him to church years ago. She hadn't explained why, and Bruno hadn't asked.

They came to the edge of the wood at last. Bruno peered out, staying hidden behind a tree, and his heart sank – the Russians were still there. The field beyond the road was a huge Russian camp, full of tents and parked tanks and Russian soldiers. He could see the burnt wagon on the road, but not Mother's body. And he knew that if he got any nearer, the Russians would probably spot him right away.

Bruno realised there was nothing he could do for Mother – a terrible thought. He felt angry and full of grief, and he told himself he should find Mother even if that meant the Russians killed him. But Frida growled softly at the sight of the soldiers, the noise bubbling up from deep inside her. She started to back off, looking at Bruno. Her brown eyes pleaded with him to come away before it was too late.

Frida was right, of course. Mother would want Bruno to stay alive, even if it meant leaving her unburied. He closed his eyes and called up a memory, a day when Mother had been happy and laughing. "Goodbye, Mother," Bruno murmured. He opened his eyes and looked out at the road and the field, fixing it all into his mind. He promised Mother that he would always remember the place where she died.

Then he turned and quickly walked away, Frida trotting along beside him.

Bruno stopped a while later to get his bearings. They were still in the wood, but he thought they could stop without worrying they'd be found. He had already decided he would stick to Mother's plan – they would head west, towards Kiel and his grandparents. But there was no point trying to catch a train.

"It looks like the Russians have got between us and the station at Königsberg, Frida," Bruno said. He was sitting on an old tree stump, studying his map of Germany. "So we're going to have to walk, at least until we get a lot further from here ..."

Bruno and Frida walked all that day, and the next. The roads were full of refugees – people fleeing from the Russians with their wagons. So Bruno and Frida kept to the woods as much as possible. They saw more Russian attacks, more blood and death, more villages burning, more smoke rising into the sky. On the second night they found an abandoned barn to sleep in, and on the third night, an empty hut.

The loaf of bread was long gone, and Bruno was beginning to feel very hungry. On the fourth day Frida went hunting and killed a rabbit, but Bruno had no way of cooking it, and he couldn't face eating it raw. Every so often a wave of grief would consume him, and Bruno would cry quietly for a while. Yet he kept trudging onwards with Frida.

Towards sunset he realised they were lost, so Bruno stopped to think at a place in the forest where two paths crossed. It was snowing again, and he was shivering. He got out his map, but he couldn't seem to make any sense of it. He was too cold.

"We can't go on like this, Frida," Bruno said, his teeth chattering.

She looked at him, head on one side, as if she were saying, *What are we going to do then?*

"We need food and proper shelter," Bruno went on. "But I don't know where to go, which path to take ..."

Frida didn't hesitate. She took the path on the right and trotted off, her nose to the ground and her tail wagging. Bruno followed, hurrying to keep up with her. The path grew narrower, the trees closing in above him, and Bruno began to feel uneasy. At last they came to a clearing with a thatched cottage on one side. Beyond it Bruno could see a chicken coop, and he heard some hens clucking.

An old woman came out from behind the cottage and into the clearing. She had a lot of white hair tied back in a bun. She was wearing a long black dress, a thick woollen shawl and an old pair of men's boots. Frida trotted up to her. The old woman looked surprised but not afraid. She put down the basket of firewood she was carrying and stroked the dog. Frida wagged her tail happily.

Bruno walked over, and the old woman turned to look at him. She had a fierce face and green eyes. Suddenly Bruno felt like young Hansel in the old fairy tale. Was this woman a witch about to eat him?

"What do you want, young man?" she demanded.

"Please, can you help me?" he said. "I'm so cold."

Bruno knew his life depended on her answer.

Chapter 4

Nothing But Hate

The old woman turned out to be much nicer than she looked. She let Bruno and Frida into her cottage and sat Bruno on a stool by the fire, building it up with the wood from her basket so that it blazed. Frida lay beside him, and the old woman fed them both – a bowl of vegetable soup with bread for Bruno, a dish of scraps for Frida. The cottage was very cosy, with a sitting room, two bedrooms and a small kitchen.

"I'm sorry if I sounded suspicious," the old woman said. Her voice was gentle now. "These are dangerous times, and you have to be careful. What's your name? And where have you come from? I'm sure you're probably just trying to keep ahead of the Russians. I've been very lucky so far – they haven't come past here yet."

Bruno answered the woman's questions. He told her what had happened to Mother, how he and Frida had found each other, and how Frida had chosen the path that had brought them to her cottage. Tears were running down his cheeks when he had finished speaking. The old woman squeezed his hand and gave him a handkerchief.

"We find ourselves in evil days and no mistake, Bruno Beck," she said, shaking her head. "But as I always say, we should help each other in this life, so you can stay here till things get better. I'll make up a bed, and we'll talk more tomorrow."

The warmth of the fire made Bruno feel very sleepy. By the time the bed was ready, he could barely keep his eyes open. The old woman left him alone while he took off his coat and the rest of his clothes. Then he slipped beneath the covers. He felt Frida jump on the bed as sleep swept over him like a dark wave …

The next day Bruno found out all about the old woman. Her name was Frau Rosa Hoffmann, but she said Bruno should call her Oma, the German word for Granny. Oma's husband had died a few years ago. Her daughter had got married and moved away before the war, to a village near Munich in the south of Germany. Oma's two grandsons were in the German Army, and she worried about them constantly.

Oma was kind and practical. She cleaned Bruno's coat and washed his clothes, giving him an old dressing gown of her husband's to wear till they were dry. She kept Bruno well fed too. There were a dozen chickens in the coop, so she had plenty of eggs. She kept a few pigs and a cow for milk, and she grew all sorts of things in her vegetable garden. Bruno hadn't eaten food this tasty for ages, not with rationing.

In those first few days, Bruno was just grateful to be there. He ate and slept and sat by the fire, trying not to think of Mother still lying out on the road. He wondered if the Russians had taken pity on her and buried her ... But that thought made him cry again. Frida came and sat beside him with her head on his knees, staring at him with her soulful eyes.

On Bruno's third day at Oma's she got him to go outside and help her in the garden. It was cold, but the sky was clear and pale blue, and Bruno enjoyed being in the fresh air. Oma asked him to sweep away the dirty snow and dead leaves that had piled up in the bad weather. Bruno could almost put everything out of his mind for a while. Frida trotted off, and he soon heard her snuffling in the forest undergrowth.

"So, what's your plan?" said Oma, pausing in her work. "You can stay here as long as you like, but I'm guessing you've got family to go to somewhere."

"My grandparents are in Kiel," said Bruno. "Mother and I were heading there."

"Kiel, you say?" Oma said, raising her eyebrows. "That's a long way from here."

Bruno knew they were both thinking the same thing. It was a *very* long way, and there would be many Russians between Bruno and where he wanted to go ...

Later that day two Russian fighter planes flew over the forest. Bruno wondered if they were the same two that had killed Mother. He ducked, his heart racing, but they were soon gone. He heard explosions in the distance and saw a column of black smoke rising into the distant sky.

They heard more explosions in the evening,
but they were even further off. No Russian
tanks came blasting through the forest.

"The Russians will stick to the main road,"
said Oma after they'd eaten and were sitting by

the fire. Frida was asleep in front of it. "That's good for us, and for the village on this side of the forest. But our luck won't last for ever. The war is nearly over, and we've lost. You mark my words, Bruno – from now on we'll be ruled by the Russians, the British and the Americans. Germany is finished, and it's all that idiot Hitler's fault ..."

Bruno couldn't help looking behind him, even though he knew nobody else was around. He had heard people in the village complaining about Hitler. But Mother had told Bruno not to listen and not to repeat any of it. She had really believed in Hitler, almost right up until the Russians had invaded. Besides, it was dangerous to say anything against him. You could easily get reported to the secret police.

"Oh, don't look so surprised, Bruno," said Oma. "I've never liked Hitler and his stupid Nazi party with their swastikas and flags and uniforms. I used to say to my husband, it will all end in tears. It's been nothing but hate ever since we Germans voted Hitler into power. Hate for other countries, hate for anybody who didn't agree with Hitler, and especially hate for the Jews. They've had a dreadful time of it."

"At school they told us the Jews are our worst enemies," said Bruno.

He thought about the horrible cartoons of Jews as ugly, evil people that he and his classmates in the village school had been shown. Herr Schmidt, their teacher, had said the Jews were always plotting against the German people. Germany had lost another war twenty-five years ago, and Bruno had often heard the Jews being blamed for that. It was something he had grown up with and accepted. But Oma thought differently.

"That's rubbish – a lie made up by Hitler and his party," Oma said. "The Jews are people just like us, and they're just as much a part of Germany. Sure, there are a lot of Jews in other countries too, but what's wrong with that? Live and let live, that's what I say."

That night, Bruno brooded about what Oma had said as he lay in bed listening to her snore in her room. He was to hear a lot worse about Hitler in the months to come.

Chapter 5

Blood on Our Hands

Days passed into weeks, and weeks passed into months, and Bruno didn't leave Oma's cottage. He often thought about it and told himself he should continue his journey to the west so he could be with his grandparents. But Bruno had everything he needed for the time being, Frida was happy, and the world outside the forest was a scary place. He knew that for a fact, from listening to the radio each evening.

"The news was bad all the time, so I stopped bothering with it," Oma said when she got the radio out of a cupboard a few days after Bruno arrived. It was a small shiny black box with a square speaker panel and a tuning dial that glowed. "But we should try to stay informed."

The news was worse than ever, thought Bruno – or at least it was if you were German. They listened to RRG, the German national broadcaster, but Oma soon said it was all Nazi lies. So she tuned in to the BBC instead – British radio. Bruno knew that doing so could get you arrested by the secret police, but also that lots of people did it. The BBC had newsreaders who spoke German, and Oma said they told the truth.

In February, they heard about the bombing of Dresden, a city in the east of Germany. It created an enormous firestorm in the city, and thousands of people were killed – many were those who'd been fleeing from the Russians.

In March, the British and American armies crossed the river Rhine in the west, and in April the Russians crossed the Oder River in the east. They attacked Berlin, Germany's capital city, and a terrible battle went on there for days.

Then, on 1 May, Bruno and Oma heard some amazing news. Hitler had been hiding in a bunker in the centre of Berlin, but now he was dead. Bruno could hardly believe it – Hitler had been the leader of Germany since before he was born. It was like the end of the world, and Bruno felt strange about it. A few days later they heard that Germany had surrendered – the war was over at last.

"Well, thank goodness for that," said Oma. "Perhaps things will start getting back to normal now. Although I don't think the rest of the world will forgive us Germans."

"You don't need to be forgiven, Oma," said Bruno. Frida was sleeping beside him on the floor. "You've never been a Nazi, and you didn't do anything bad."

"Ah, but we Germans gave Hitler power, Bruno, so the world thinks we all have blood on our hands," Oma explained. "And many Germans have done truly terrible things."

Bruno knew what she meant. They had heard reports on the news about camps in Poland and Germany that the Russians, British and Americans had found. The Nazis had rounded up Jews and other people in many countries and sent them to these camps. There they'd been starved, beaten and killed by poison gas. Millions of men, women and children had been brutally murdered and their bodies burned in ovens.

Bruno just couldn't believe what he was hearing when it had first been reported on the radio. How could anybody treat others that way? He knew people often did terrible things in war, of course – like using dogs as suicide bombers. But the camps were different – as Oma said, that was pure evil. Yet it had happened, and now the names of the camps kept going round and round in Bruno's mind – Dachau, Treblinka, Auschwitz …

Then he started to wonder about his parents. Mother had believed in Hitler, and Bruno knew that she had wanted Germany to win the war. What if Father had helped to capture people who were sent to the camps? What if he had been a camp guard and killed innocent people? He had been in Poland and other places where there were camps ...

Bruno talked to Oma about it, and she told him not to be too hard on his mother. Oma had been shocked by the camps but not surprised – she'd always known the Nazis were evil. "Plenty of people were fooled by Hitler," Oma said. "And I'm sorry to say it, Bruno, but you might never see your dad again. I suggest you try to believe he was a good man and steered clear of all that evil. I hope my grandsons did anyway."

Bruno listened to Oma, but it didn't help. At night he lay in bed brooding, unable to sleep even with Frida cuddled up close beside him. He still felt deeply guilty that he had left Mother behind on the road. But now Bruno also felt guilty about all the people who were dead because of Germany. It felt as if his parents were to blame somehow. And if they were gone, perhaps he'd have to take on their guilt as well.

But Bruno didn't say any of that to Oma. She was quite cheerful. Spring had come and the sun was shining. To Bruno the clearing in the forest seemed more like an enchanted place from a fairy tale than ever. They knew from the radio that the Russians were everywhere in the east of Germany, and their planes often flew over. But for some reason not a single Russian – or anyone else – came to the clearing.

One day in June Bruno felt restless, so he went walking in the forest with Frida. Bright rays of sunlight shone down between the branches, and for a moment Bruno felt that it was good to be alive. After a while they came to the other edge of the forest, near the village Oma had mentioned. It reminded Bruno of his own village, and he felt a pang of sadness as he looked out at the houses.

Then he saw that there were Russian soldiers in the village, and he was filled with fear. The soldiers were banging on doors and yelling at the villagers. They forced them out of their homes and into the open space before the church. The soldiers surrounded the terrified villagers, pointing their guns at them. Frida growled and Bruno moved her back into the shadows beneath the trees. He couldn't take his eyes off what was happening.

Another man stepped forward. He was clearly with the Russians, and he had a rifle and a pistol in a holster. But he was wearing a white shirt and dark trousers, not a Russian uniform. He started speaking – in German but with a Polish accent.

"This village is no longer German," the man shouted. "It belongs to Poland now. You all have one hour to leave – unless you want to be buried here, that is."

There were gasps from the villagers, and an old woman started moaning. Bruno saw that the crowd was mostly old men and women and mothers with children.

"But this is our home!" another woman called out. "Where can we go?"

"Who cares?" said the man, shrugging. "You Germans have to pay for the evil you've done. If we were like the Nazis, we would shoot you and be done with it!"

Then he fired his rifle up into the air, and the villagers screamed.

Bruno and Frida ran back through the forest to Oma.

Chapter 6

The Road of Tears

That evening, Oma and Bruno listened to the radio. They moved the dial round and round, tuning into as many different stations as they could. But the news was the same on most of them. Germans in the eastern parts of the country were being forced to leave. Areas that had been German for hundreds of years were being claimed by the Poles and the Russians. And there was nothing the Germans could do about it.

"Well, I reckon we only have ourselves to blame," said Oma. "If you treat people badly, they'll do the same to you when they get the chance. We tried to take their lands, and we killed a lot of them. Now they're just taking their revenge."

Bruno knew Oma was right, but he was still upset by what was happening. There were reports that Germans who refused to leave were being killed. He also kept worrying about what the woman had said – where could the villagers go? At least Bruno had a plan, somewhere to aim for. But what about the people who had nowhere to go, nobody to give them shelter? Then another worrying thought occurred to him.

"The Russians and Poles will come here too, won't they, Oma?" Bruno said.

"They probably will, but I'm not going anywhere," she said. "I'm far too old to leave my home and become a refugee. No, they'll just have to shoot me."

"Please don't say that, Oma!" Bruno said. He could feel tears prickling in his eyes. "We could leave together! You should go to your daughter! Frida and I will make sure you get to her."

"I'm sorry, Bruno, but my mind is made up," said Oma. "But you should definitely leave – you've got your whole life ahead of you! You should leave tomorrow. I'll help you get ready ..."

The next day, Bruno found out there was no arguing with Oma. Every time he talked about Oma leaving with him, she changed the subject. Eventually he gave up. Perhaps the clearing in the forest where she lived was truly enchanted, he thought. The Russians and Poles didn't turn up, and Oma spent the day calmly sorting out Bruno's clothes. He began to wonder if he should stay with her after all – but Oma simply wouldn't hear of it.

"Don't be daft, Bruno," she said in the morning. "You should have gone a long time ago. Your grandparents are probably worried out of their minds about you."

"Well, if you're sure ..." Bruno said. He was outside the cottage, with his rucksack on his back and Frida beside him. The sun was shining and the only sound was the clucking of the hens. "I don't know how to thank you for all that you've done for me."

"There's no need to thank me, Bruno Beck," said Oma. She was standing in the doorway, smiling at him. "The food should last you a good few days, and I'm sure you'll manage after that. And you should get in touch with my daughter anyway."

"I'll try, Oma, I promise," Bruno said. Oma had written her daughter's address on a piece of paper and made him put it safely in his rucksack. "I'll be off then."

Bruno gave Oma a kiss on the cheek and quickly walked away. Frida followed, but they both stopped at the edge of the clearing and turned to wave. Oma waved too, and Bruno decided to fix that picture in his memory – of a smiling Oma and her cottage.

He had a terrible feeling that he would never see her again.

And so began the last part of Bruno's journey to the west. He stuck to the forest as much as he could at first. But eventually his map told him he would have to take to the road. Bruno came out of the trees and saw that the road was filled with people – an endless group of refugees. They were mostly old men and women, mothers and children. Some pushed carts or prams, but many had nothing other than the clothes they wore.

"Well, this doesn't look good, does it, Frida?" Bruno murmured.

Frida found his eyes with hers. *But we don't have any choice*, her expression seemed to say.

"You're right, as usual," Bruno said. "Come on, let's go. Maybe things will get better ..."

Bruno and Frida joined the refugees, and for a few days they trudged along the road to the west. He soon thought of it as The Road of Tears, because he saw so much weeping. At every village and town they passed, Bruno

saw people being forced out of their homes.
Sometimes there was shooting and people
were killed. And many others died of hunger
or sickness on the road, mostly the old and the
very young.

The days passed into weeks and then into
months. Later Bruno remembered only the
things that stood out. Things like crossing
a battered bridge over the river Oder and

walking through a battlefield on the road to Berlin, with burnt German tanks and unburied bodies everywhere. In Berlin itself, almost every building had been destroyed, and gangs of women were clearing away rubble while Russian soldiers looked on.

Bruno saw other ruined cities and met many people on his long journey to the west – some good, some bad. Frida could always tell who to avoid and who to trust, pulling him away or drawing him closer. Twice Frida saved Bruno from being robbed and hurt.

They found many places to sleep – abandoned farms, bombed buildings, in the woods when the weather was good enough. After Oma's food ran out they lived on what they could find, or went to the food distribution centres that began to appear along the road. The first one Bruno saw was run by British soldiers, so he knew they'd arrived at last in the west.

Just as Oma had said, Germany had been divided up by different countries, and Kiel was in the British sector. Bruno and Frida came to the city on a cold and rainy day in November. There was some bomb damage, but the city didn't look too bad, and Bruno began to feel hope rising in his heart. He asked a man for directions to the street where his grandparents lived but had to ask someone else before he found it. He could hardly believe that his long journey was nearly over, and that he and Frida had survived it.

Bruno turned a corner – and saw that the street had been totally flattened, including his grandparents' house. Where it had stood was now just a heap of rubble. For a moment Bruno stood staring at the smashed bricks and broken beams, feeling all his hope drain away. Then he sank to his knees and lowered his head. The rain dripped off the end of his nose and down his front. Frida moaned softly and licked his face.

"I'm sorry, Frida," Bruno whispered to her. "I don't know what to do now."

And deep in his heart Bruno couldn't help feeling it was somehow right that his story should end this way. He was a German, so he was sure that he didn't deserve a happy ending. After what the Germans had done in the war, how could there be anything for them in the future but guilt and shame? Everybody hated the Germans, even the British soldiers who had given him food. He had seen it in their eyes.

He noticed that Frida wasn't with him any more. He turned round and saw that she had run up to a grey-haired woman in a shabby old coat. Frida was wagging her tail, but the woman was hardly taking any notice of her. Instead she was looking at Bruno with her eyes narrowed as if she couldn't believe what she was seeing. But then he could understand that. He couldn't believe what he was seeing either.

"Bruno ...?" the woman said at last, her voice shaking. "Dear God, is it you, Bruno?"

"Yes, it's me," he said to his grandmother, and soon they were hugging.

His journey was over, and the rest of his life could begin.

Chapter 7

Full of Life

Kiel, Germany – October 2015

Seventy years later, Bruno Beck stood in the doorway of his house and looked down the street. It was late in the afternoon and the sky was grey, but he had something to look forward to. His young granddaughter was coming to visit, and he couldn't wait to see her.

"Come inside, you old fool," said Katrin, Bruno's wife. "You'll catch your death of cold standing there like that. Besides, it won't make Maya get here any faster."

"I know," said Bruno. "I just got fed up sitting there watching the TV. It's awful, what's happening in Syria. Seeing all those refugees brought back a lot of memories. But that will help Maya, I suppose. She said she wanted to ask me about the past ..."

There was so much to remember, Bruno thought. He was old now – eighty-one on his last birthday. His bones creaked and most of his hair had gone, and the face he saw in the mirror every morning sagged and was covered in wrinkles. But in his heart he was the same boy who had stood in another doorway seventy years ago. Sometimes it felt as if that was yesterday, and Bruno wondered where all the years had gone.

Maya arrived at last, kissing her grandfather on the cheek. Soon she, Bruno and Katrin were sitting at the kitchen table, eating cake and catching up. Maya was sixteen and Bruno loved seeing how full of life she was. Her lovely brown eyes were just like his mother's, Bruno often thought.

"So let me tell you about my school project," said Maya after a while. "We're studying the Nazis and the end of the war. The idea is to find out what it was like for German refugees, and if they suffered like the people fleeing Syria today."

The war in Syria had been going on for a while. Cities were being bombed and thousands of people had been killed. Hundreds of thousands of people were fleeing, trying to get to the rich, safe countries of Europe, such as Germany. That meant they had to cross the sea in small boats, and many were drowned. Some countries were refusing to take in the refugees, and there had been lots of trouble on their borders.

People had argued about it in Germany too. There were some who thought they shouldn't allow so many refugees into their country. But then Chancellor Angela Merkel, leader of the government, had simply told everyone to stop worrying. "We'll manage," she'd said, and now thousands of refugees were being welcomed all over Germany. She remembered Germany's history, Bruno thought. She understood.

"Well, I'm not the one to talk to," said Katrin to Maya. "I'm a few years younger than your grandfather, and I don't remember much about the war. I was lucky too – I lived with my parents on a farm near the Danish border, so we were never refugees."

"I knew that, Oma," said Maya. "And I know you *were* a refugee, Opi."

Maya had always called them Oma and Opi, German for Grandma and Grandpa. Bruno had never really thought about it before. But today the word "Oma" conjured up memories of a magical clearing in a forest and the smile of an old woman.

"Yes, I was a refugee," said Bruno. "And I do remember those days very clearly."

They talked for ages, and Maya made notes. Bruno told her about the day he and Mother left the village and she was killed when Russian planes attacked. He told Maya about leaving Mother behind on the road, and making friends with a Russian suicide dog.

"I can't believe that," said Maya, shocked. "Did they really do that to dogs?"

"They did, but then all sorts of terrible things happen in war," said Bruno. "It was lucky for me that I met Frida. She saved my life many times, and I still miss her ..."

Bruno felt a pang of sadness as he thought about Frida. She had lived another eight years after the war, and, like him, she had settled down happily with his grandparents. They had been given a couple of rooms in a house for homeless people after their house had been destroyed. Later they had moved to another house, where Bruno had spent his teenage years. When Bruno was nineteen, Frida had died peacefully in her sleep of old age.

Bruno told Maya the rest of his story – about staying with Oma, the Russians and Poles forcing Germans to leave their homes, and his long trek across a shattered Germany.

"It must have been terrible, Opi," said Maya. "How did you feel about it?"

"Oh, that's an easy question to answer," said Bruno. "I felt guilty – when I found out what we had done to other countries, and especially to the Jews. I still do."

"But *you* didn't do anything wrong," said Maya. "So you shouldn't feel guilty."

"Well, I did feel that way," said Bruno. "And I also felt I should do something to make up for what Germany had done. I think a lot of people my age felt much the same."

"That's why your grandfather became a doctor," Katrin told Maya. "He always wanted to help people, and I'm very glad he did. I wouldn't have met him otherwise ..."

Bruno smiled, remembering how he and Katrin had met at medical school – Katrin had been a doctor too. The first few years after the war had been tough, but Bruno did well at school and university. He had been very proud when he finally became a doctor, and he had always thought that Mother would have been pleased. He was also sure she would have made a wonderful grandmother to his daughter, Monika, and son, Günter.

Bruno's father never came home. Bruno tried to find out what had happened to him, but most of the German Army's records were destroyed at the end of the war. He did discover that Father's unit was fighting in Poland at the end of 1944, and that it was almost completely wiped out in a Russian attack. Bruno hadn't wanted to know any more, in case he discovered that Father had been involved in doing something bad.

Bruno never found out what happened to Oma either. He had written a letter to Oma's daughter, but she didn't reply. Bruno told himself the Russians and Poles might have let Oma stay in her enchanted clearing. He liked to think so anyway.

"Thanks, Opi. I think I have all I need now," Maya said eventually. "I didn't realise what you'd been through. It really was as bad for you as it is for the Syrians now."

"I survived and had a good life," said Bruno. "Maybe we can make sure the Syrians do too. And maybe one day the rest of the world will learn the lesson we did."

Bruno stood in the doorway once more when Maya left, and he watched her walk down the street in the autumn twilight. She turned and waved, then was gone.

He went back in and shut the door behind him.

It felt good to be in his home.

Historical Note

At the end of the Second World War, millions of Germans living in the eastern areas of the country became refugees. Nobody knows exactly how many Germans left their homes or were forced out, but it was at least twelve million and might have been a lot more. Many died as they fled, but again the exact figure isn't known – some historians think it could have been between half a million and six hundred thousand.

It was a terrible thing to happen, and it came after the most terrible war in human history. But it isn't something that many people outside Germany know about. In Britain, we talk about the Second World War a great deal, but we learn about it from our point of view. That means we tend to see the Germans as the villains – and there's no doubt that Adolf Hitler and his Nazis led the German people into a huge war that caused great destruction and suffering. But that doesn't mean that the entire German population were to blame.

It's understandable that the people of other countries found it hard to feel sorry for the German refugees, or see them as victims. But when I began to learn about everything that had happened, I realised the refugees were old people, mothers and children. You could think badly of the adults perhaps – many of them voted for Hitler and supported his Nazi party. But how could the children be blamed?

Germany committed great crimes in the Second World War, but it paid a terrible price for them. Most German cities were flattened by bombs, and the whole country was devastated.

It was split into occupied zones, which later became two separate countries – East Germany and West Germany. West Germany recovered and flourished again, but the story was different in East Germany. The Russians controlled that country until the fall of the Berlin Wall in 1989. The government of East Germany was very hard on the people – the secret police there watched everybody all the time.

East and West Germany were reunited in 1990, and Germany is now one of the richest and most successful countries in the world. But the Germans haven't forgotten their past – children are taught in school about the awful things Hitler and the Nazis did. Germany has also tried to make amends for the terrible things that were done. German leaders have often said sorry for what their country did in the war. Germany has also paid lots of money in compensation to the countries it attacked, and also to Israel, where many of the Jewish survivors settled after the war.

So I wasn't surprised when Germany led the world in tackling the refugee crisis in 2015. Hundreds of thousands of people were fleeing the dreadful civil war in Syria, together with those running from other troubled parts of the Middle East. Many of the refugees wanted to go to Germany, and the country took in nearly a million people in the end. To me it showed just how far Germany had come – and also that people and countries can learn lessons and do better.

And let's hope one day that there will be no more wars, and nobody will have to be a refugee.

Our books are tested
for children and young people by
children and young people.

Thanks to everyone who consulted on
a manuscript for their time and effort in
helping us to make our books better
for our readers.